The Tales of
The Chosen

The Tales of The Chosen – 1st ed.

By Matthew Faulkner

This is a work of fiction. The names, characters, places, and events are either products of the author's imagination or are used fictitiously, and any resemblance to actual persons, living or deceased, business establishments, events, locales is entirely coincidental.

ISBN-13: 978-0-615-77858-7

ISBN-10: 0615778585

Printed in the U.S.A

Cover Art Design by Brittany Ungvarsky

For my parents,
Rita and Scott Faulkner

Chapter 1

It was a dusty morning where the second sun had risen before the first. The Institution of Learning was expecting to receive a reward for their 1400 years of consecutive perfection. The rulers were pleased to see their minions moving about so seriously, as the display of emotions was strictly forbidden at the Institution of Learning. The Chosen were taught at a young age to swiftly complete their studies. Each week they were given pills that fed a Chosen member for a seven-day period of time.

After the seven days, the individual was reevaluated to see if he or she were keeping up with the required study of knowledge. If an individual did not meet the level necessary for that week, they would starve for one week until they proved themselves by subsequent week's judging. The "Intellectual Elite" made all the decisions. The design for the Institution of Learning was state of the art. The interior was equipped with high-tech security cameras, motion sensors, and twenty-four hour patrols at all entrances and exits. The exterior, on the other hand, had been weather-worn over the past 1400 years since the great war but in its prime, no one could crack it. The exterior was equipped with reinforced concrete walls, guard towers that reached one hundred feet high, missile detection systems, electrified chain-linked fences with chicken wire wrapped, but their greatest defense of all, was the fact that no one could reach them. They floated miles high in the sky using stolen technology. The Intellectual Elites spared no expenses but as the years went on, the rules and protections originally in place were greatly relaxed. Even still, they were cruel monsters that feasted upon the finest meals from around the world. They hardly knew or could understand what the Chosen were even learning, only that their ancestors in the past used this knowledge to create a powerful world of wealth and harmony. The Intellectual Elite were evaluating one of their minions when, all of a sudden, shouting broke out, there were three Chosen boys bad-mouthing a girl named Cherry.

The three Chosen boys thought it would be hilarious if they knocked Cherry down over the railing. They wanted to show off to all their friends watching how strong they were. There was a crowd around the boys cheering them on. "Do it! Do it!" the crowd shouted.

Cherry's friend, Rye, tried to grab her while she was hanging onto the railing but the boys did not want him to ruin their fun so they proceeded to punch and kick the boy named Rye in the eyes, legs, arms, and chest relentlessly. The crunching sound of his bones could be heard echoing through the hallways as Rye continued to help Cherry up.

The crowd, once cheering, paused in the shock from the sound of broken bones. They all quickly looked at each other until one boy shouted, "I am not getting in trouble with the guards," and quickly ran into a nearby room to avoid the incoming guards towards the scene. The boys kept screaming and laughing, "Look at this fool!"

Rye continued to hold Cherry's arms for dear life. Rye was finally able to pull Cherry up to the very edge of the railing so she could hold onto the metal safety rail securely. Then Rye's face turned very red and angry. For the first time in his 274-year-old-life his primal thoughts surpassed his intellectual teachings. He'd grown wild and fought back with his legs kicking them in the face and chest. Through his powerful blows from his martial arts teachings, his kicks crushed two of the kids' ribs into their hearts, killing them instantly. The other boy screamed for his friends and made a temporary retreat. It was then Rye immediately pulled Cherry back up from the dangling 173-mile drop.

Rye could feel the two suns beaming on his face forcing him to block the light with his hands. Then out of nowhere, a fourth boy showed up and stabbed Rye rapidly in the chest with a three-inch boot knife he'd stolen from a guard. Surprisingly, Rye drop-kicked the kid in the face knocking him unconscious and launching him across the room into the safety railing in which the boys had recently thrown Cherry over. Rye then looked down at the knife in his chest. Seeping around it was a waterfall of blood.

He then turned his attention to Cherry and asked, "Are you okay? Did they hurt you?"

As Cherry began to respond Rye's vision began to fade and his feet started to give way. While Rye started falling to the ground, he attempted to grab Cherry's shoulder for support. As Rye began to fall farther to the floor, Cherry grabbed him by the hand and then shoulder to slow him. As Cherry began to survey the area, she saw the pool of blood around Rye's body. She then screamed, "Call a medic!" But the panicked crowd around her drowned her voice out, plus the guards were too busy to even notice what was happening.

Cherry began checking Rye's vitals and airway to make sure he was not choking on his own blood. She kept screaming, "Help! Help! Somebody help!" until there seemed like there was no hope left.

She had her hand around Rye's wrist feeling for his pulse, and every minute that passed the softer and slower Rye's pulse became. After the medics finally arrived, they took him to the hospital. While Rye was being taken away, Cherry insisted on being in the ambulance with Rye. Cherry needed to hold Rye's hand, to feel for a pulse.

When they finally got to the hospital the security guards and hospital nurses were forced to physically detach Cherry from Rye's side. After twelve long hours of surgery and sixty expensive cups of coffee, the doctors finally came out of the urgent care room. They began to talk to Rye's parents. Cherry quickly ran over to hear what the doctor was saying.

The doctor said calmly, "Excuse me ma'am, I have some bad news…"

This is all Cherry needed to hear; she began to walk away in tears. Her feet began to grow weak. Eventually, she collapsed back in her seat in a loud uproar of sorrow towards the sky. Cherry's parents began to comfort her as she cried for hours on the way back home. Cherry went to his funeral that weekend and placed a white rose in his coffin, she muttered, "This is not fair..."

She felt alone. Cherry was depressed for weeks after Rye died. Her studies were starting to slip week after week. The Intellectual Elites began to take notice and summoned her to their chambers one day. They were not pleased at all.

Chapter 2

Cherry knocked on the Intellectual Elite's chamber doors softly. The door then opened on its own slowly and a firm and loud voice from the room commanded her to come up. As she walked through the doors, they slammed shut behind her. Cherry jumped in the air a little when she heard the doors close. She then paused in place and turned back towards the metal and oak doors.

The moment her eyes laid on the door behind her, an extra metal door went over the original door preventing it from being opened again by hand. Brian, the leader of the Intellectual Elite, commanded, "Come here, Cherry!"

She reluctantly began to walk forward towards Brian. Once Cherry got close enough towards Brian, he asked her, "Is there something wrong Cherry? Can you explain your recent behavior?"

Hesitantly, Cherry began to mumble but only gibberish came out. Brian became increasingly frustrated with her lack of response and screamed, "Answer me!"

Cherry blurted out, "Rye!" and then Brian paused for a moment.

He made a confused face and then looked towards one of his advisors. A tall, thin man with brown hair and a gray suit walked over to Brian and whispered in his ear. Brian then said, "Thank you. Explain yourself, Cherry! How does Rye have anything to do with your performance with your Chosen studies? You are here to work and anything less than perfection will not be tolerated!"

Cherry slowly and reluctantly responded, "I … I … cared about Rye and now he is gone. It makes me sad—"

Mid-sentence Brian screams, "Sad? What do you mean sad? It is forbidden to display or feel emotions, Cherry!"

Cherry interrupts, "But you are…"

Then Brian continues, "Maybe you need time to reevaluate your life. Lock her in isolation. Oh, and no food for a month! You will be whistling another tune, Cherry, ha-ha."

Cherry begins to panic and her throat begins to tighten. Her breathing becomes panicked, "Wait, I am sorry. I did not mean to!"

Brian sat back down on his throne-type of chair made of ripped up coach cushions from the war. Then he started a lovely conversation with one of his assistants next to him and ignored her. Then a moment later as Cherry was watching Brian, many servants came up to him to hand-feed him rich expensive food such as grapes or bananas.

"Take her away!" Brian screamed while laughing.

Cherry let out a chaotic scream, "No, no wait!"

It took three well-built guards to drag her tiny, kicking, and screaming body away, and one more just to open the door to let them out.

Brian began to smirk and let out a snicker, "Now that she is out of the way, bring in the next slacker! There will only be perfection in this Institution."

Cherry's scream could be heard down the hall as many people around her paused to watch her get dragged away. This is a pretty common yet sad sight at this

Institution. It is a feared sight as well, because it is a reminder of what happens to those who do not achieve absolute perfection.

Everyone knows what is going to happen to her in the study room downstairs, she will be brainwashed of these newfound emotions and put back into service at the Institution. Cherry is dragged through many doors and bumped against doorframes and walls kicking and screaming until the guards get fed up with her constant resistance. They smash her on the head with a metal rod. Her vision begins to go dark and she passes out.

Chapter 3

Cherry wakes up to a rattling of chains and screams from down the hall. She quickly opens her eyes; they are at first fuzzy but become clear quickly. Cherry becomes frantic and looks left and right only to see metal bars and stone walls. She then attempts to stand up but finds the radiating pain from her head unbearable and sits back down. She then notices the chains around her arms and legs.

In a plea of desperation she tries to rip them off with no luck. The three-quarter-inch reinforced iron shackles were too much for her to remove. Cherry then started to look around even more and noticed she was in a very small cell no bigger than five-feet across and six-feet high. The lighting from the ceiling is very dim, except for the bright electrified bars creating constant flashes of light every now and then. The flooring was made of old-fashioned bricks. It is pretty clear where the Institution dumps all the "free money" they receive for producing really smart Chosen. The thought of a system where the Chosen are leased out for material exchange made Cherry sick. All of a sudden Cherry jumps, she noticed a flash of light from down the hallway and she begins to hear voices talking. She starts to lean closer to her bars without causing her shackles to make too much noise. She starts to overhear their conversation, "Man this is the fourth time this week," said Paul.

"No kidding, I mean what is happening? Is the software failing?" said Steve.

"Let's hope not, that's more work for us anyway. Who is it this time?" said Paul.

"Some crazy girl who cannot stop thinking about some dead guy," said Steve.

A sense of fear begins to vibrate up her feet and through her spine; she becomes frozen in fear. Her thoughts began to run wild in her mind. What are they going to do with her? What do they mean by "software" anyway? Her thoughts are stopped in their tracks at the sight of the two guards.

"Well, hello there," said Steve.

Cherry begins to shake her restraints rapidly in a failed attempt to become free. "I hope you're not trying to escape, that's platinum!" said Paul.

Both men begin to laugh.

"You just sit tight, dear, we will take care of you in a few minutes," said Steve.

Both men start to walk away laughing. Cherry jumps forward to try to see where they are walking to but the length of her shackles halts her. She then begins to slowly sit back against the rough concrete wall behind her wondering what will happen to her. It's difficult for Cherry to concentrate because she is both physically and mentally exhausted from today's ordeal. She slowly begins to pass out from the shock of all these events.

Chapter 4

Cherry hears Computer beeping and metal scraping sounds. She slowly starts to open her eyes and she sees bright lights, which causes her to close them abruptly. She attempts to reopen them again but this time blocks the light with her hands. As she starts to do this, she is quickly halted by the tugs on both her arms. She finally squints and sees she is in restraints again but this time in a room with bright lights and beeping computer noises. She tries to shift her head to the left and right but she cannot. Her head is firmly mounted in a metal frame that obscures her view and prevents her from moving. It is a gold-plated frame that has a slight polish on it.

Cherry can see a dim reflection of her pale face. It has a slight shiny glimmer but days of no maintenance have taken its toll. She has bags under her eyes and bruise marks on her face from when she was dragged away. Some of the bruises were beginning to turn purple, and she notices a faint tear coming slowly out of her left eye.

She then hears a howl of pain from Steve, the guard, who has hit his head on the doorframe.

"Watch where you're going!" said Steve.

"No! You watch it. I am pushing the back here. This generator is heavy, you know!" exclaimed Paul, the other guard.

Cherry instinctively tries to sit up to see what's happening but gets stopped by her restraints. "What do you mean? How can I watch the front if I am walking backwards?" said Steve.

"Oh great," whined Paul.

Steve began to turn his head towards the front, "What?" said Steve.

"There goes our quiet morning," said Paul as he looks towards Cherry.

"What are you going to do?" Cherry asked curiously.

"Fix you," said Paul.

"What!" Cherry screamed.

"Calm down, girl, I just woke up," Steve grunts.

"We are going to fix you, for good, especially that hair of yours, Cherry," Paul snickered.

"Wait, what's wrong with my hair?" said Cherry.

Steve grunts and wipes his hand down his face.

"Really, Paul?" said Steve.

"Well you know with some of that new shampoo they just came out with ..." said Paul.

"Just start the generator," said Steve.

"Fine, starting the generator," exclaimed Paul. Paul's head begins to shift down towards Cherry and whispers to her, "I will get you some afterwards."

The sound of the loud generator begins to roar and she begins to hear beeping noises bouncing between her left and right ear. She hears the generator start to ramp up to speed.

"Start the prog—" Steve stops talking abruptly.

"What happened?" asked Paul.

Smoke begins to appear around him and he makes a loud grunt. Cherry tries to look around but cannot, then all of a sudden her head is free along with her body and she is being carried off. She starts to look up but the thick smoke is blocking the person's face. She hears him scream, "Blow the doors!" but it couldn't be him. It couldn't be him.

Chapter 5

Cherry hears water dripping; she hears drop after drop hit the puddle of water on the floor. She begins to open her eyes and sees a small lantern light above her head. She starts to sit up and suddenly she sees and hears Wanda say, "Easy there, girl, you're still injured."

Cherry slowly begins to lean back as Wanda is propping up the pillow behind her back.

"Where am I?" Cherry asks.

"Don't worry, your safe, Cherry!" exclaims Wanda.

"Safe where?" Cherry quickly asks.

"Safe and sound in an underground bunker. You're lucky we got to you in time, they were about to wipe your memory," explains Wanda.

"What do you mean my memory?" asks Cherry.

"Oh you don't know? The Intellectual Elite have been doing this ever since the accident," says Wanda.

"What accident?"

"Well, around 2500 years ago, I think. There was a military arms race, the threat of war was ever looming, and our country was tricked into fueling this race. Then one day, they had done it; they built this new type of bomb that promised remarkable results but, as usual, they never tested it. They decided to just try it when their country was threaten, but it turned out to be too remarkable; the bomb split the planet into three pieces," said Wanda.

"Wait, what?" said Cherry.

"Yes, in three pieces, only a very small part of our planet remains. Then, fifty-six years later, the Intellectual Elite took over promising our original lifestyle back. All you had to do was get reeducated at their school first," said Wanda.

"Wait so everything I know—" Wanda cuts off Cherry.

"Yes, yes, I have said too much. You will need to rest up for tomorrow. You have a big day ahead of you," says Wanda.

Cherry slowly begins to close her eyes and falls asleep. She begins to think to herself. "A lie?" Cherry whispers as she slowly begins to fall asleep.

Chapter 6

Cherry wakes up to a beeping sound, she slowly opens her eyes to find a very dark room. In fact, it looks like a cave. She sees a drop of water hit the ground and looks up at stalactites on the ceiling. She then looks down towards the ringing noise and sees an old-fashioned phone.

She starts to get up and walk away from the phone and down the hall. She sees different color pipes above her head towards the top of the ceiling. The lighting in the hallway was very dim with a lantern every twenty feet. As she begins to walk she feels the rough rocky floor against her bare feet and she sees a closed door every ten feet.

As she continues to walk down the hall she hears a loud noise from one of the rooms. She begins to lean in against the door and hear a slight muffle but then suddenly the door she is leaning on opens and knocks her backwards towards the hard rocky floor.

The room was filled with seven to eight people. The first person she sees is Gingerbread, and she can also see Wanda towards the back of the group. Cherry is lost in a trance of Gingerbread's eyes and unexpectedly blurts out, "Rye?"

"What? No, who are you?" replied Gingerbread.

Wanda quickly answers, "Oh, that's Cherry. You know, the one we saved."

"Oh, I can see why my brother had a crush on you now," said Gingerbread with a smile.

Cherry quickly asks, "Wait! You're not Rye?"

"No, we're all escapies from that dreaded Institution of Learning," Gingerbread softly replied.

Cherry's face slowly begins to fade.

"He never told you? Well, get up now, we have places to go!" Gingerbread energetically replied. He gently grabs her arm and slowly pulls her up from the floor. "No shoes?" Gingerbread asked.

"No," Cherry answers.

"Who has shoes? Cornbread, I need your shoes, man, both of them!" Gingerbread screams.

"My shoes?" said Cornbread.

"Yes, your shoes, hurry now, it won't kill you."

Cornbread hesitantly begins to take off his shoes and starts to hand them to Cherry but Gingerbread grabs them before he can give them to Cherry.

"Size thirteen shoes? Way to be there when I need you, Cornbread." Gingerbread throws Cornbread shoes back at him while Wanda hands Cherry some slippers.

"It will have to do, let's go," said Gingerbread disappointedly.

Cherry begins to follow Gingerbread, Wanda, and Cornbread down the hall. The hallway seems to go on forever and Cherry becomes horribly lost in which way they have taken her. After a long while of walking, Cherry sees a dimly lit latern begin to appear farther down the hall. Once they arrive at the lantern they entered the room where the lantern was hanging above the door, everyone in the room pauses and salutes them.

Gingerbread replies, "At ease, friends. Commander, what do we know about the school?"

The commander replies, "Well, they have tripled the number of guards in and around the school. They have increased their number of patrols in and out of the school. They have also cracked down on the Chosen in the hallways if they start a scene. Plus, they have changed their passwords again so it will be awhile before we can use their camera feeds again."

"Very good, Commander," said Gingerbread.

"Why don't we just go in there and free them all?" asked Cornbread.

"We don't have enough people, Cornbread. Do you know how many we lost just to free Cherry?" said Gingerbread.

Cherry begins to think to herself, lives lost because of me? How many?

"Sir, if I may?" asks the Commander.

"Go ahead," says Gingerbread.

"I was running simulations and if we plant bombs on the main four generators we could cause the school to have a major power loss. They would not have enough backup power to keep the school afloat and in the chaos we could easily swoop into the schools and destroy the gates that keep the Chosen trapped. From there, we could make a series of raids on the school to free all the Chosen. We have plenty of rooms down here for them to live away from those evil Intellectual Elite."

"Wouldn't the school crash land? Anyone left inside would die," asked Gingerbread seriously.

"It is possible," said the Commander.

Gingerbread slowly placed his hand on his head to massage his nose. "Alright, let me think about it. Commander, you are in charge until I get back. Let's go, team!" said Gingerbread.

"That's all of us," Cornbread elaborates while pointing to Cherry and the rest of the group.

Cherry and Gingerbread exchanged a look, and they all began to walk back down the hall.

"You've seen nothing yet. This place has an amazing selection of food," said Gingerbread.

"Don't forget about the desserts!" Cornbread adds.

As Cherry begins to listen to the conversation between Cornbread and Gingerbread she begins to grow faint and becomes a little dizzy. Wanda notices right away and grabs her by the arm and helps her carry on. Cherry begins to hear her stomach growl. "I hope they're right about that elaborate selection of food," said Cherry.

"Just wait and you will see, dear," Wanda replies.

Chapter 7

Cherry and Wanda finally arrive at the two brown double doors with circular glass windows in them. Cherry pauses a moment staring at the two doors wondering what she will find behind them. Who will be there? Will they accept her? All of a sudden, Wanda gives Cherry an abrupt push.

"No time to think about it, just eat, eat! You're so skinny," said Wanda happily.

Cherry catches herself by landing on the doors, which suddenly gave way in front of her. She cannot stop herself from moving forward. She is stuck between not wanting to enter the cafeteria and wanting to. This sudden confusion has caused her legs to lock up and she starts to plummet straight towards the floor. Her eyes begin to widen as the black and white tiles begin to come clearer and brighter. Her vision begins to fade and she wakes up in Gingerbread's arms. Her eyes open to a bright ceiling light above her head, and she swiftly blocks it with her hand. She starts to sit up on the floor and begins to hear Gingerbread's voice echo and multiply in her head, "You know how to make an entrance."

Cherry quickly shoots back, "What?" in a lost tone but after a moment Gingerbread's voice becomes clear.

"Well, don't let the doors jump in front of you next time," Gingerbread replies with a smile.

Laughter begins to fill the entire cafeteria. This is the first time Cherry notices the hundreds of people standing around them eavesdropping on the conversation. They both start to get up and head towards the cafeteria line while walking over, the different smells throughout the air begin to fill Cherry's nose. She starts to smell flapjacks, pasta, pizza, bananas, apple pies, fish, cooked pears, tuna fish, along with freshly baked bread, and much more. She is so overwhelmed at the sight of all these different foods. She did not even know

what some of the foods even were. She
decides to play it safe and just grab a plate
with tuna fish, green beans, and mashed
potatoes. All of a sudden, Gingerbread lays
a slice of apple pie on top of her plate
covering all of her food.

"You could use the calories," said
Gingerbread.

Cherry replies quickly staring into his
eyes and hesitantly says, "Thanks."

Once she picked up her plate of food
and her newly acquired slice of apple pie
she turned around to find a place to sit. She
sees tons of people sitting around
Cornbread and Gingerbread. She quickly
turns away towards a quieter table but

stops. She begins to hear Wanda calling her over and she calmly walks towards her.

"So, how do you like the place?" asks Wanda curiously.

"Which place? The cafeteria that has food I have never seen before? The War Room with a bunch of flashy lights and a crazy general, or a hospital room with a single lantern for a light?" exclaims Cherry as she is running out of breath.

"Well, first off, the general's name is Trizzy, and he is my husband," explains Wanda.

"Oh, ummm, yeah. Nice guy!" Cherry exclaims with a smile.

"I meant, how do you like the people here?" says Wanda.

"They're okay, I guess, nothing too major to report." Cherry stares at Gingerbread's face for a moment.

"Really, now, nothing to report?" asks Wanda.

"Nope, hey, wait. Why didn't Rye tell me about Gingerbread?" Cherry quickly replies.

"Hard to say," says Wanda.

"Did you know Rye?" Cherry asks with heavy confusion.

"Rye, used to lead this place until he died on duty," expressed Wanda with a bit of sadness in her throat.

Cherry begins to stare down at her mash potatoes and begins to spin them around with her fork. She starts to remember back to when the doctor told her that Rye would not make it. She visualizes his funeral and seeing him lay there in the coffin. Suddenly, tears begin to fall from her eyes and Wanda quickly catches her shoulder and says, "It is going to be okay."

"No, it's not!" Cherry screams while knocking Wanda's arm away.

She then stands up in her chair knocking it backwards onto the floor causing everyone around her to stop and stare for a moment. She runs straight for the door shoving people aside. Some of them had food in their arms, which now covered the floor.

Chapter 8

Cherry's sobs can be heard down the halls and echoes throughout the entire cave for miles. She eventually stops when she finds the maintenance shed with no one in it and leans against the back wall. About fifteen minutes later Gingerbread shows up.

"How did you find me?" asks Cherry as she wiped tears from her face.

"Well, it was not hard to follow your path of destruction," said Gingerbread.

They both begin to look back and see knocked over shelves, medical supplies thrown on the floor, and clothes from nearby linen closets scattered everywhere.

Cherry continued to clean her face off with part of her t-shirt.

"What's wrong?" asks Gingerbread.

"They killed Rye, I know they did. The kids who attacked us, I have seen them before. I am certain they were out to get me. I hate that stupid Intellectual Elite guy known as Brian! Who does he think he is giving himself such an annoying title? He seems dumb to even have that name. Why did they kill Rye?" said Cherry as she began to run out of breath from talking.

"I think they found out he was an undercover agent for the Muffins," said Gingerbread.

"The Muffins? What are you saying? He likes to eat food?" asks Cherry.

"No, 'The Muffins' is the code name for our underground organization. We had to pick a name we could pass around in a school without raising suspicion," said Gingerbread.

"Oh, I can't believe he is gone. You know, you look a lot like him. Your hair is a little different but your eyes are the same," said Cherry as her mouth began to form a smile.

Gingerbread begins to blush a little and then looks away towards the sky. "Yeah, we are twins so that tends to happen. I don't like this though, my stupid brother," said Gingerbread.

"Your brother?" asks Cherry.

"Brian is my brother," said Gingerbread.

"Your brother, I cannot believe he killed his own brother! Did you steal his girlfriend?" said Cherry.

Gingerbread lets out a long sigh, "It's not like that Cherry. He became messed up after our mom died. It is not your fault; he was just a really strange kid. I always wondered about him when we were growing up, mom was too before she died, of course," said Gingerbread with a frown.

"That's terrible! How long have you known about this? What are you going to do?" pondered Cherry.

"A long time," moaned Gingerbread

"Who knows about this?" asked Cherry in a curious tone.

"Me, you, Rye, Wanda, and Trizzy," said Gingerbread.

"You should do something, you should stop him. What are we going to do?" says Cherry.

"What can I do? Kill him?" asked Gingerbread.

"Look, you are worlds different from that guy. Someone like him and his evil ways—he has no regard for human life. You clearly do, that's why you can't kill him. You just need to do something and not just sit around here. Just take him out for the good of the world or whatever is left of it," said Cherry as she grabs his shoulder and shakes him.

"I won't have any family left then," said Gingerbread in a very sad tone.

"Brian took your family from you," said Cherry. She then stares at Gingerbreads face for a moment and blushes. She quickly turns away before Gingerbread would have time to notice. Gingerbread begins to tilt his head up towards Cherry's face.

"You will have me, Cornbread, Wanda, and Trizzy. Don't forget Rye," said Cherry as she pointed to Gingerbread's heart. Gingerbread looked up at her face and stared into her eyes. His face began to tear up. He reached forward then hugged her. A few moments later Gingerbread says, "Thank you."

"We should probably go, we have one-third of a world to save!" exclaims Cherry using a humorous tone in an attempt to cheer Gingerbread up, but it did not work.

Gingerbread begins to wipe his face off. Cherry exclaims, "Hey, I thought you came here to cheer me up? Not the other way around."

"What are you talking about? This was my three-step process of cheering you up," said Gingerbread with a positive tone.

"Three steps?" Cherry asked.

"Yeah, step one, find you," said Gingerbread. "Step two, cry." Cherry laughed. "Step three, save the world." Gingerbread laughed.

Cherry began to laugh with him and they both stood up.

"Let's go work on a plan," said Gingerbread.

"Actually, can we stop and get some food along the way? I am starved," says Cherry as she looks into his eyes and laughs a little.

"Sure, it's not like millions of people's lives depend on it. No problem," said Gingerbread with a strange tone.

Cherry's face lights up. "I will race you!"

"Wait, this cave floor is uneven and there are some sharp spots along the way you can trip on," said Gingerbread.

Cherry then pushes Gingerbread away and makes a run for the door. Gingerbread takes notice and grabs her arm as she starts to run.

"Where are you going?" Gingerbread begins to laugh.

Cherry quickly replies, "Cheater!"

Cherry quickly attempts to pull her arm free from Gingerbread but he holds onto her arm and is knocked off his balance. He begins to stumble towards the door falling towards Cherry's back. The weight of Gingerbread knocks Cherry forward.

"What are you doing? Stand up already!" Cherry complains.

She begins to shove him off and start to crawl towards the door. Gingerbread is just starting to regain his balance and sees Cherry quickly taking the lead. He quickly reaches out and grabs her leg but Cherry kicks his hand off. She then quickly stands up in the doorway of the room out of breath and exclaims loudly, "I win!"

Gingerbread quickly remarks back, "You are such a cheater."

"I'm the cheater? You're the one trying to slow me down!" said Cherry.

Gingerbread is now just beginning to stand himself up off the dirty cave floor. He begins to recompose a serious face. "Let's go," said Gingerbread.

Chapter 9

Cherry begins to take note of his serious face and tries not to laugh. They continued walking down the long corridor with its dim lighting and rocky interior.

"Would it kill you to put a window in here?" asked Cherry.

"We are in a cave for your information. Just be glad we have a deal with the traders nearby to get something decent to eat," said Gingerbread.

"Oh? Digging miles underground and reinforcing it with a single glass window won't work?" said Cherry sarcastically.

"Oh yeah, let me just dial an 800 number and get it fixed today. No, but really, we are like flat broke. Well, technically, we never actually paid for any of this. It was just left over from the last uprising. The place was in complete disarray though. We had to fix everything. Even the televisions were broken!" said Gingerbread.

"Oh my goodness, not the television! Call the cops! What will we do without television, when there was never anything on to begin with?" Cherry joked.

"Hey, hey, there is nothing like watching those *House* reruns from thousands of years ago. All ten seasons of fun! You will be surprised how boring it is down here," said Gingerbread.

"Well, you will be surprised how boring it was up there," said Cherry pointing up towards where the floating school might be.

"Yeah, good point, I guess. What did you do for fun up there?" asked Gingerbread.

"Fun? What is fun? We had to work sixteen-hour days and we only got eight hours of sleep!" said Cherry. "Wow, only eight? We at least get twelve hours here."

"Well, we didn't have a choice. Otherwise, you would be punished by the guards," said Cherry.

"What did they do?" asked Gingerbread with slight hesitation while he was thinking of his brother Brian.

"Well, for starters, they were not nice. If you made eye contact with them or bumped into them they would hit you with their electric batons. If you really got out of line, they would make an example of you. The entire Institution would be forced to watch the person being whipped or being thrown into the gym full of lions. It was so sad and you could not do anything. Some people seemed to enjoy it," said Cherry.

"It is a shame Rye couldn't be here telling us about this," uttered Gingerbread

"I bet. I don't know how he got into there but no one escapes the Institution of Learning."

"Hey, Cherry! You're safe here, don't think about those things anymore. I am sorry I asked," said Gingerbread as he shook Cherry's shoulder.

"Okay," said Cherry. She looked up towards to his hand on her shoulder and then to Gingerbread's face. After few seconds she broke her focus.

"We should go."

They both continued to walk down the hall towards the cafeteria and heard yelling and glass breaking. This immediately caught Gingerbread's attention and he ran towards the cafeteria door. He quickly pushed it open to see what was happening only to find Cornbread fighting with another civilian.

Gingerbread began to scream, "Hey! Hey! Stop it! What are you doing? Stop fighting! What is wrong?"

Neither Cornbread nor the man he was fighting would listen to him. Gingerbread was forced to run towards the fight and break up the brawl. After a few minutes of tackling both of them to the floor he got completely fed up and punched them both in the face. The crowd paused in disbelief. They couldn't believe what he had just done.

"What is the matter with you two? Why are you fighting?" said Gingerbread.

As Gingerbread completed his sentence and started to look towards the man Cornbread was fighting, Cornbread

tried to make a pass at the man.
Gingerbread saw Cornbread's hand head
towards the man and he pushed Cornbread
towards a chair but Cornbread just hit the
chair and slid on the floor. "Sit down,
Cornbread, I have enough trouble running
this place," said Gingerbread.

The man behind Gingerbread began
to yell, "Well, maybe you shouldn't be
running this place!"

Gingerbread swiftly turned towards
him and recognized him. "Tom? What is
wrong with you?" said Gingerbread.

"No! What is wrong with you? This
place has been going nowhere. No official
operations have been carried out for weeks.
Our people are still trapped up there in that

terrible school! That cracked up brother of yours is driving our kids into the ground up there! That's right, I heard. It is your brother ruining our kids' lives up there. How can we trust you? Maybe you're just trying to suppress us too!" said Tom as he pointed towards himself then towards the crowd watching.

The crowd moaned in response to Tom's statements about Gingerbread. "What in the world or you talking about? Who is feeding you all this nonsense? I am trying to run this entire place while keeping everyone safe and fed before bedtime. I have good news though: we have made a break through. We now have inside intelligence on the layouts and the structures, and we are developing a plan right now to take the place down once and for all! This fighting is not helping one bit!" said Gingerbread.

As Gingerbread began to look around at the crowd he saw the faces of anger and fear be put to rest. "I'm sorry, Gingerbread, my vision was clouded," said Tom as he began to put his head towards the ground.

"Don't look down, mate, we can do it. Have you got those old engines working yet?" said Gingerbread

"Umm, almost. We are missing a few parts," said Tom.

"Okay, see what you can do. We have another shipment coming in today. Let's saves some lives people!" said Gingerbread.

The crowd began to talk amongst itself. There was a new wave of hope spreading throughout the crowd. Finally, their prayers for hope have been answered.

Chapter 10

Gingerbread grabbed Cherry's arm and pulled her towards the cafeteria doors. "Wait! Where are we going?" asked Cherry.

"We have much to do, to the War Room, Cherry," said Gingerbread.

Gingerbread continued to hold Cherry's arm until they both get outside of the cafeteria.

"It's not easy, huh?" asked Cherry.

"No, it's not," said Gingerbread in a slightly exhausted tone.

"So, where is this new inside intelligence going to come from?" asked Cherry.

"You," said Gingerbread as he paused for a moment to say his message and then quickly walked away from Cherry.

"What?" exclaimed Cherry. "You have walked day in and out inside those halls. You know what everything looks like, how they run their guard patrols, and more importantly, who likes to slack off," said Gingerbread as he walked alongside her.

Cherry began to think to herself, Gingerbread was right. She begins to recall the guard who seemed to disappear for fifteen minutes or so and come back smelling like smoke. The Elite never seemed to care about breaks, and the thought of a union was such a joke. Anyone who started any type of organization was always publically executed for the whole school to watch. They would even stop the whole Institution of Learning to show everyone.

Gingerbread began to wave his hand in Cherry's face. "Hello? Is Cherry in there? Alright, now start thinking. What rooms did they not allow you to go in?" said Gingerbread.

"Well, the janitor's closet or the offices they worked in usually. I know of a guard that takes an unscheduled lunch break for fifteen minutes every day," said Cherry.

"Good! Good! Show us on the map; this is the evil brainwashing school. Commander Trizzy, pull up all the janitor closets," said Gingerbread.

"Oh yeah, sometimes the guards play a game of cards while on duty inside the closet while classes are going on. They are supposed to be patrolling the halls to make sure everyone is in class but the Elite never give them a break," said Cherry.

"Okay good, is it this closet right here, Cherry?" said Gingerbread.

"Yeah, I think so. Wait! No, this one is it," said Cherry.

"Okay so this one?" said Gingerbread, as he marks a red X on the blueprints.

"Oh second thought, maybe this one? No this one. Wait, wait, it has to be this one. Sorry, I cannot remember. I am not used to doing anything like this," said Cherry.

Gingerbread takes the marked up blueprints and stares at the eleven red Xs and says, "It's okay Cherry, this kind of narrows it down," as he moves the blueprints to the middle of the table and then put his hand on her shoulder to comfort her.

In the background, both Gingerbread and Cherry, the military men and women are hard at work holding the map up and moving it around trying to find the north heading. Both Gingerbread and Cherry can hear a man in the background ranting about the eleven different Xs they would have to investigate to find the right spot to hit before the attack on the Institution of Learning.

Cherry began to look up towards Gingerbread and then quickly looked away after Gingerbread whispered something in her ear. Cherry began to pull away from Gingerbread some and looks towards the ground. Gingerbread quickly took the hint and removed his hand.

"Alright, we finally know who likes to slack off. Commander Trizzy, please pull up all the guards ever posted at that spot. What are their patrol times?" said Gingerbread.

"What spot? She marked eleven of them," said Commander Trizzy.

"Is it not obvious? Clearly the only spot with a vending machine next to it would be where they would hangout," said Gingerbread.

"What is a vending machine?" said Commander Trizzy.

"You know, you put money in the machine and you get some item you want out of it," said Gingerbread.

"That sounds very unhealthy, how would you get your daily vegetables out of it?" said Commander Trizzy.

"Are you a vegetarian?" said Gingerbread.

"For the past 200 years, yes," said Commander Trizzy.

Gingerbread pauses for a moment then says, "Just curious, did you put that petition on my desk for more vegetables in the cafeteria?"

"There are thousands of vegetarians at this base, it could have been anyone," said Commander Trizzy as he winks at Cherry.

Gingerbread takes notes of what Commander Trizzy just did and says, "Moving on, patrol times, let's go!"

"Let us see, we have 9:30am, 1:15pm, 5:55pm, and 10:20pm at this vending machine, sir!" screamed Commander Trizzy as he emphasized the last five words.

Cherry unexpectedly blurts out, "10:20pm! I know that guard falls asleep on the job around that time," said Cherry with a loud voice that gradually gets quieter as more and more people begin to look at her.

"How would you know that? Do they not force everyone into their rooms by 5pm?" said Gingerbread curiously.

"Well, I may have sneaked out from time to time to take some extra food pills from the refrigerators," said Cherry in a sneaky tone.

"Stealing, Cherry? I thought they raised you better. Oh wait, they didn't. Just a heads up: that is wrong. Anyway, it is decided then, 10:20pm or so we sneak in through the maintenance shaft

82

conveniently connected to the one janitor closet that Cherry pointed out and place bombs on their main generators. From there, once the place crashes we can send in ground teams to rescue the Chosen and maybe that vending machine. Who knows, maybe it will have vegetables in it," chuckled Gingerbread as he stares at Commander Trizzy.

"But wait, they have really advanced sensors they stole from the underground bunkers from the times of the war. How are we going to sneak in? We have no advanced air craft," said the man standing next to Commander Trizzy in a textbook manner. "Okay, keep it simple, people. Who knows, maybe those devices do not work anymore. Stop being so negative," said Gingerbread.

"No, they still work," said Cherry.

"Okay, plan B, just hang glide in and since they do not like to waste power running spotlights. No one will even see us come in. Too small for radar and it will be too dark for them to see with their naked eyes," said Gingerbread.

"But they do run spotlights at night," said Cherry.

"Alright, no one panic! Plan C, come with me to the storage below. I have a very good idea," expressed Gingerbread in a sneaky tone.

"Well, if you put it that way. What could we have to lose?" said Commander Trizzy.

Chapter 11

The people in the room with Commander Trizzy and Gingerbread began to make a loud roar of support for the current idea at hand. Commander Trizzy begins spouting out orders left and right. People around him start notifying the flight teams to report to the garage.

This all became so surreal for Cherry, the audio around her begins to blend together and her hands start to shake. She begins to stutter backwards and bumps into a person walking behind allowing her to catch her balance for a moment. Her knees begin to grow weak and she hits the floor with both her knees and hands. Gingerbread hears the sound of her hitting the floor and turns his head towards her and quickly runs to her. He runs back behind her to try to stand Cherry back up.

"You know, we need to get you out more, Cherry. Someone call Wanda! It will be okay, Cherry," said Gingerbread.

Cherry's eyes began to close and her face started to become very pale. Cherry began to hear snapping around her ears, "Wake up. Cherry, can you hear me?"

Cherry began to open her eyes but she only saw a very blurry image of Wanda,

"I do not feel so good," moaned Cherry.

"Why is this happening?" asked Gingerbread.

"Well, I just did a blood test and it's not good," said Wanda.

"What is she a diabetic? Don't we have something for that?" asked Gingerbread.

"No, it's not that simple; I think it is a lysine deficiency," said Wanda in a worried voice.

"Lysol? Is that not a cleaning product?" said Gingerbread.

"No, this is serious, Gingerbread. She has a lysine deficiency, this means she is missing essential amino acids," said Wanda.

"Well, what do we do? Do we have a pill for that or something?" said Gingerbread.

"Well yes, but it is not that simple. We have not had a medical shipment for the past month now. Ever since our bunker on the bright side of the earth was raided last month, we have been short on everything and all the nearby traders have gotten too scared to trade with us," Wanda.

Gingerbread began to fall backwards in shock. "Could she die?"

"Yes, by the looks of it. Wait, where are you going, Gingerbread?" said Wanda.

"Watch over her, I know where the medicine she needs is," yelled Gingerbread as he begins to grab the machine gun by the bed and check its ammo.

"Don't worry, I will watch over her. She needs you, Gingerbread," said Wanda. Gingerbread ran out of the room and towards the planning room.

Along the way he runs into one of his men and says to him, "Hey, turn around and tell everyone in the hanger change of plan. Tell them all to wait for further orders in the garage."

The man seems shocked and quickly ran off towards the hanger.

"Trizzy! Trizzy! Where are you?" blared Gingerbread inside the war room.

"Right here," said Trizzy.

"We need to load up the secret weapon," said Gingerbread.

"What? Are you crazy? We have not tested it nor do we have a person who knows how to pilot it," expressed Commander Trizzy.

"Well, time to take her out for a spin," verbalized Gingerbread as he began to press on a keypad by his chair.

"Wait, who is going to fly it?" asked Command Trizzy.

"Who do you think?" said Gingerbread.

Commander Trizzy began to take a deep breath and started rubbing his temples on his head and said, "Happy thoughts, happy thoughts. I will make it to 5pm. I will make it."

In the meantime, Gingerbread began to run out the door with a pair of old-fashioned keys and headed towards the flight deck. Once he arrived there he grabbed a megaphone and screamed, "Everyone stop! Change in plan, guys, we are getting there in style. Open the doors, Commander Trizzy. What do you see there, boys and girls, is a 1952 crop duster equipped with cushion seats designed to support your back. We have also equipped these with windshield wipers and a mounted machine gun for all your airway needs. We are going to raid the Institution of Learning tonight," explained Gingerbread.

"Where did you get these? A museum?" asked Command Trizzy.

"Maybe, does it matter? The fact is, we have them. Let's go people! All you have to do is move the little metal steering wheel to control it. Oh and don't get shot down. I have no clue how to fix these things," said Gingerbread sarcastically.

"Oh, great way to really rally the troops, Gingerbread," whined Commander Trizzy.

"Oh and press the little button to turn the engine over. Any questions?"

asked Gingerbread as he pointed to the button on the plane.

"Yeah, umm, what's a crop duster?" asked a young member from the crowd.

Gingerbread paused. "Well, I think it was used to—not important, just press the button and move the metal steering wheel around. Let's go!" shouted Gingerbread.

The crowd and the room began to disperse and load up into the different aircrafts they pulled out from the hanger. They had two to three men and women pushing open the both hanger doors so the planes could take off.

"On my mark men, 3, 2," Commander Trizzy was interrupted.

"Just go people! We have lives to save. Go, go, go!" screamed Gingerbread.

As he quickly took off others followed him towards the Institution of Learning. Gingerbread's heart began to change on the inside, and he quietly whispered out loud to himself, "You're not my brother anymore, Brian."

The rest of the planes from the hanger began to converge around Gingerbread's crop duster. The noise the planes made could be heard for miles.

Command Trizzy came on the radio, "We believe with this electrical storm coming in, it should mess with their shields and allow some shots to make it though. Aim for the towers with the bright beacons on them. Once they are all destroyed we will parachute down and invade that crazy Institution of Learning."

His voice stops because Gingerbread interrupts him, "Once you find Brian, he is mine. No one kill him, we are going to bring him back alive, is that clear?"

Commander Trizzy comes back on, "Stand down, Gingerbread, listen to me. Try to conserve your ammo; we still don't know how to actually make bullets yet."

"Make what? Are we not using metal bullets?" asked Gingerbread.

"No, it is some type of plasma round we found in Area 51," said Commander Trizzy.

"Well, that's good to know. No pressure, guys."

Chapter 12

"Oh wait! Is that it?" asked Gingerbread.

The planes barreled towards the floating rock. They first noticed the high rising walls around the intuition. The cracked concrete walls and weather-worn exterior had seen better days. The sight of the place reminded Gingerbread of his past, visiting his father at the local jail. He never liked going there; his mother always forced him to go so he would seem supportive. Along with Gingerbread, Brian and Rye would go visit as well. They would always spend an hour or so there every Wednesday night, the only night when there were no good shows on the television.

"Gingerbread, Gingerbread! We are here!" yelled Commander Trizzy repeatedly.

Gingerbread looks up right as a bolt of lightning flashes in the background, the complete outline of the building is lit up for a spilt second and then goes dark again. Gingerbread's eyes begin to turn dim and un-alive.

"Open fire," Gingerbread said softly.

All the planes began to break formation and surround the Institution and a shower of molten bullets begin to rain down. The concrete towers got taken down one by one exploding outward in many different pieces with little to no resistance.

"It seems we caught the guard off guard. Time to go on foot," said Gingerbread.

Once Gingerbread touched ground he tossed a few grenades to break down the doors in front of him. His troops in the sky quickly join him after the doors exploded open. They ran inside with guns pointed in all directions only to find that the lights were hanging from the ceiling flickering on and off. There was a large amount of paper scattered around on the floor and the lockers were covered with bullet holes. The floors were littered with dead or dying school enforcers with their white uniforms stripped of their weapons and armor.

"What happened in here? Did someone beat us to the punch?" said Gingerbread.

"Maybe," said one of his troops.

Gingerbread turned towards his troops. "You know they could have called us or made a smoke signal," teased Gingerbread.

"Maybe they did? We live underground you know," said the man next to Gingerbread with a serious face and a cracked smile in the corner of his mouth.

"What was that?" hollered Gingerbread.

The entire group stops talking and held their breath. They all slowly started turning their head to the right but then the piercing sound of a pin dropping echoed throughout the hall. Gingerbread quickly turned his head along with the other soldiers in the group towards the left and started to look at Tom, the talker.

"Really, Tom? All you ever want is attention, man. Okay, what was I doing again?" said Gingerbread.

"Saving the world maybe?" said the man next to Gingerbread.

"Oh right, that explains the gun."

Chapter 13

"To the right, let's go!" said Gingerbread after looking left and right.

They all quickly ran towards the right jumping over trash and blown out bits of drywall on the floor. The worn-out red paint on the school lockers, mounted on the wall, brought up tears from Gingerbread's past, but he was quick to wipe his eyes before anyone noticed.

As they travel farther down the hall they heard a radio playing opera music, and as they get closer they saw a door sitting open with light shining from it. Some men quickly rolled past the open door and braced on the opposite wall, guns drawn.

On the other side of the door from his troops, Gingerbread took a defensive position on the outside of the door.

The men all watched Gingerbread's hand as he counted down from three to zero with his fingers. Once his hand reached zero they stormed in the room with guns drawn at shoulder height. They noticed a sleeping old-timer propping his legs on the dashboard of the controls. His chair was leaning back with two of the old wooden legs off the ground. The men then noticed the blinking red alarm on the screen that read: "Perimeter breach," but no sound is playing.

Gingerbread lowered his gun down to his side and leaned towards the man to reach the control panel. As Gingerbread reached over and nearly presses the button to turn the alarm off; the old man leans over towards the door and kicks Gingerbread in the face causing Gingerbread to let out a loud grunt.

As the old man's feet start falling towards the floor he grabs a pulse rifle mounted under the control counter and begins to aim the pulse rifle towards the people behind Gingerbread. A moment later Gingerbread recovers from the blow to the face and aims the old man's gun towards the ceiling. As Gingerbread is moving the gun the old man begins shooting. Bullets hit a fire alarm sprinkler on the ceiling causing water to flow from the roof, flooding the room. The soldiers behind Gingerbread start racing towards the fight scene until an explosion behind them knocks everyone to the floor.

Gingerbread and the old man fly towards the wall in front of them. As Gingerbread's vision recovers from the blast he begins to sit up. His ears begin to ring and he finds the old man had been knocked unconscious under him. Gingerbread slowly starts to sit up and see his soldiers on the floor not moving. He quickly jumps towards the closest man to him and begins to shake them.

"Tom? Tom! Ugh, why!" said Gingerbread as he shifted his head from left to right. His focus on the scene is broken from the bullet fire down the hall. "Uh oh!" Gingerbread screams and tears begin to fall down his eyes from the thoughts of his fallen men and women. He slowly begins to reach down towards Tom's ammo pouch to grab a few rounds from his gun. As he sits up he closes Tom's eyes and whispers, "Never will forget you."

He looks at all his fallen soldiers now dead on the floor then quickly runs towards the door as he hears new rounds of bullets fly. He begins to poke his head out the door and quickly leans his head back. As he is pulling his head back in the room a bullet grazes his right cheek. Gingerbread then feels the side of his face as blood begins to pour.

"Oh man, how many are there?" Gingerbread asks himself out loud. He then quickly darts towards the old man's control panel but trips over a fallen comrade on the floor. When he sits up, he hits the back of his head on the underside of the control console. He twists his head around towards the left and starts to look up and sees three smoke grenades mounted under the counter with a thin metal strip holding them in.

"What is this guy's deal?" says Gingerbread aloud in an exaggerated tone. A second later, he jumps to the floor at the sound of more explosions. The shockwave from the blast keeps Gingerbread pinned to floor under the control panel. He closes his eyes. He reopens his eyes and sees a picture frame near him.

"Employee of the month. I can see why," said Gingerbread as he tossed the frame towards the unconscious old man on the floor. Gingerbread then begins to hear men shouting orders outside of the room he is in.

"Time to go," said Gingerbread as he grabs the smoke grenades and throws them towards the door. Then he goes for the pulse rifle the old man had only to find it was too damaged to use. Gingerbread quickly looked back at the door then again back into the room. He starts to frantically look around until he sees an air vent mounted on the wall.

Gingerbread begins to consider his options out loud, "Should I go into a small dark cramped air vent or should I run down a hall way showered in bullets?" When he hears a few rounds fly pass the door, Gingerbread jumps. Then he begins to shout, "I have always wanted to go through an air vent!"

Gingerbread runs towards the air vent. He begins smacking the air vent with a computer chair over and over again. The men outside begin banging on the door attempting to break it down.

"Just a second! I am opening the door!" shouted Gingerbread as he frantically hits the vent cover over and over again. When the vent finally gives way he jumps into it and throws a smoke grenade behind him as he hears the men break the door down. The walls around Gingerbread are cramped, and he finds himself slithering through the air vents like a snake.

Chapter 14

He finally reaches another air vent cover on the other side. Conveniently, he notices Commander Trizzy through the small holes in the air vent and calls to him. "Trizzy, help! No, look the other—no, man, to your right. Break this thing open, I am stuck," whined Gingerbread.

"Gingerbread, what is wrong with you? Why are you in an air vent?" asked Commander Trizzy.

"It is a very long story, we need to find Brian and shut him down. Wait, who are these people?" asked Gingerbread as he stares at some new faces.

"These little guys are ten years old. They also attacked the same time we did and put the heat on Brain," said Commander Trizzy.

"So let me get this straight, a bunch of kids with no organization or strategy were able to just stumble upon some equipment and infiltrate a highly fortified base with little to no training?" asked Gingerbread.

"We're not just kids. We just walked in and no one stopped us. I guess they figured a bunch of ten-year-olds weren't a threat. I mean, how badly could 200 hundred kids wreck a generator room full of important wires? All we did was press every button. We got a high score too, the red lights were blinking!" shouted one of the lads.

"What is your name?" asked Commander Trizzy.

"My name is Mint, and we call ourselves the Junior Mints! No parents allowed though, remember that!" said Mint.

"The Junior Mints? Really? Hey, do you guys know where Brian is at?" asked Gingerbread.

"Do you mean that big mean guy who yelled at us for messing up their stuff? He's holed up in the gym. Something about a power failure and this whole place is going to come crashing down. I kind of zoned out about the rest," said Mint.

"Wait, what? Did he say how long?" asked Commander Trizzy quickly.

"I don't know, hey do you have any candy? I want some candy," said Mint.

"There is no time for candy. Wait, Something about that statement is wrong. Anyway, Trizzy, did you bring any snacks? I am kind of hungry after thinking about that candy we left at the base," said Gingerbread

"So you do have candy!" said Mint.

"At the base," repeated Gingerbread.

"Ugh!" said Commander Trizzy and he rubbed his hand on his forehead.

"Calm down, Trizzy. Okay, take us to the gym," said Gingerbread.

"Can I ask you something, mister?" said Mint as he pulled on Gingerbread's shirt, and Gingerbread begins to lower his ear towards Mint's mouth.

"The bathroom? Ummm ..." said Gingerbread as he looks left and right but saw no markings of one anywhere. "Sure, I know exactly where one is," said Gingerbread as he walks down the hall until he passed a water fountain.

"Wait, you do?" said Commander Trizzy as he begins to follow Gingerbread.

Chapter 15

Gingerbread goes to a boarded up door and wipes recent dust off the sign that reads: "Restroom" and kicks the door in.

"There, have at it," said Gingerbread.

"Thanks, mister!" said Mint as he and his friends all ran into the bathroom yelling, "Tag, your it!"

"Well then, where did they come from?" asked Gingerbread.

"I don't know," said Commander Trizzy.

"Oh and the part about when you were going to tell me?" said Gingerbread.

"Oh by the way, I found a bunch of kids who infiltrated the Institution of Learning," said Commander Trizzy jokingly.

"Well, that was really convenient for us," said Gingerbread. Kids begin to storm out of the bath yelling, "I'm done!"

After a few minutes of this Gingerbread finally said, "Okay, is everyone here? Did everyone use the bathroom? Now did everyone wash their hands?" A few kids began to slowly walk back into the bathroom.

"Hey. umm, Gingerbread? You know we are in the middle of a war?" said Commander Trizzy.

"This is why some people die, Trizzy," said Gingerbread with a long face.

"To bullets?" said Commander Trizzy.

"No, to poor hygiene, Trizzy. Did you wash your hands?" said Gingerbread.

Commander Trizzy begins to walk away from Gingerbread slowly and heads down the hall.

"I noticed you're avoiding my question. I have some hand sanitizer here!" said Gingerbread.

"Let's go already, Gingerbread," said Commander Trizzy.

"Okay. Mint, where are you? Oh there you are, lead the way," said Gingerbread.

"It is just down here, mister," said Mint. They all head down the hall towards the gym and finally reach the gym doors. Both Commander Trizzy and Gingerbread boost Mint up towards an air vent so he can see inside. "What do you see?" asked Commander Trizzy.

"A lot of people running around," said Mint.

"Anything else?" asked Gingerbread

"Well there is a lot of them," said Mint.

"Perfect, you did great, Mint. Okay, I was thinking we sneak in through the air vent and turn the power off to the generators in there," instructed Commander Trizzy.

"Oh no, you can count me out. No more air vents for me, Trizzy. I have had enough with small, dark, and cramped spaces," said Gingerbread.

"Are you claustrophobic?" said Commander Trizzy.

"No, no, this is a new suit," said Gingerbread. The both begin to stare down at Gingerbread's ripped up shirt and torn pants from the previous blast.

"Mm-hm," said Command Trizzy.

"Hey, I know. Mint, do you want to be a hero?" asked Gingerbread.

"Are you crazy? He's just a child!" complained Commander Trizzy.

"No, no, nothing too serious, just run past armed guards and pull a few cables from the wall," said Gingerbread as he gives Mint a high-five.

"A few guards?" said Commander Trizzy.

"Yeah, one, two, three …" said Gingerbread. As he proceeded to count the rest of the guards he saw on his hand, glancing back and forth at the room and then back at his hands.

Commander Trizzy crosses his arms and leers at Gingerbread saying, "Mm-hmm," repeatedly while Gingerbread was counting.

"Forty-seven!" screams Gingerbread.

"Watch and learn, Gingerbread," says Commander Trizzy as he walks into the gym and shoots the generator causing sparks to fly. The lights in the room begin to flicker and eventually go down to a hardly noticeable dim.

"Get those generators back up!" screams Brain. He then looks up to where the shot came from. "Stop him!" Brian continues to scream.

The guards begin to look up towards Commander Trizzy, they start throwing hatchets and firing lasers at him. Gingerbread rushes into the room to knock Commander Trizzy down to prevent the attackers from hitting him.

"We need to move. Mint, take you and your group and get out of here," said Gingerbread.

"But we want to help!" whined Mint.

"Just go!" said Gingerbread.

Both Gingerbread and Commander Trizzy begins to crawl next to the guard railings in hopes of not being shot. They quickly rush towards a few boxes of crates and brace their back against them.

"What do we do?" asked Commander Trizzy. All of a sudden, the lights in the room go completely out and the room is filled with screams and darkness.

"We improvise," said Gingerbread.

They both stand up and start running around the catwalks till they reach the section that is above the last generator.

"Stand your ground, men, they could be anywhere!" said Brian.

A person next to Brian begins to scream in pain and then another, and another.

"What is going on?" asked Brian.

The lights turn back on and Brian sees the Junior Mints tackling the guards around him. Around five to six kids are holding down each guard. Gingerbread and Commander Trizzy take notice and jump down near Brian.

"Gingerbread! It was you? Are you trying to destroy everything I have built? I am trying to change the world here," said Brian fearfully.

"No, you are trying to conquer it. That's why you built this terrible place, your castle floating in the sky?" said Gingerbread.

"You are coming with us, Brian," argued Commander Trizzy.

Both Gingerbread and Commander Trizzy rush towards Brian but Brian quickly jumps back and says, "No, never!"

Brian turns around and run the opposite direction while throwing crates towards both of them in an attempt to slow Gingerbread and Commander Trizzy down. Brian darts out the backdoor of the gym with the green exit sign lit up above it. Both Gingerbread and Commander Trizzy follow behind him. Once they both exit the gym a few shots begin raining down close to them on their right side far down the hall. They both get low to the ground but suddenly they hear Cherry scream, "Come on, I know another away around!"

Both Gingerbread and Commander Trizzy look at each other and then run in Cherry's direction.

"What are you doing here, Cherry?" pondered Gingerbread.

"I thought you were still sick?" urged Commander Trizzy.

Cherry gives them both a funny look and points out, "I have a lysine deficiency. I am not dying."

"But you could be dying? Oh well, we both kind of thought ..." muttered Gingerbread.

"We thought? You were the one who would not listen to me. I tried to tell you—" expressed Commander Trizzy.

"Enough. Cherry, you said you know a way around?" pondered Gingerbread.

"Is that smoke?" probed Commander Trizzy.

They all turn around and see a raging fire head towards them from down the hall.

"I got to go! I will catch you all later," suggested Commander Trizzy.

"Wait, we cannot go that way," uttered Gingerbread.

"Why not?" pondered Commander Trizzy.

"They are still shooting bullets down the hall, we'd be turned into Swiss cheese. Not the tasty kind either," howled Gingerbread.

"Well, the fire is kind of blocking the only other way I knew around. We are blocked in now," says Cherry.

"There may still be hope, the air vent!" said Gingerbread.

Gingerbread begins pulling Commander Trizzy in the direction of the air vent until Commander Trizzy says, "Oh no, I am not going into that small air vent. I am claustrophobic plus I would die of suffocation."

"Well you are going to be dead-o-phobic if you do not come," whined Gingerbread.

"It is called necrophobia, Gingerbread, and I do not appreciate you rushing me into this vent. I need to do my breathing exercises," explained Commander Trizzy.

"Oh, I am sorry, you take your time and maybe in five minutes you would have consumed all the air left to breathe in here," worried Gingerbread.

Both Cherry and Gingerbread begin to drag Commander Trizzy towards the air vent and start lifting him into it.

"I am going to die!" screamed Commander Trizzy.

"Get in there. Cherry, grab his legs!"

Commander Trizzy began kicking his feet like a small child. "Hold still!" says Cherry.

Once they shoved him into the air vent Gingerbread reached for Cherry to go through the air vent.

"Which way do we go, Cherry?" pondered Gingerbread.

"Left! Left? No wait, right! Actually, make two rights, then a left," guessed Cherry.

"Do you know where we are going?" asked Gingerbread.

"I do not exactly take the air vents to class everyday, Gingerbread. Why don't you stop and ask for directions along the way if you don't believe me," heeded Cherry.

"Maybe I will," preached Gingerbread.

"Really?" asked Cherry in annoyed face.

"No!" screamed Gingerbread as he quickly broke eye contact with her.

Chapter 16

After getting lost in the air vents for several minutes they finally decided to kick out a vent cover and jump down. They began to poke their heads out at once and struggled to decide who'd get to leave the air vents first. Commander Trizzy was more motivated than Gingerbread or Cherry.

"Let me out!" said Commander Trizzy.

"We need to check where we are first," warned Gingerbread.

"Any place is better than in these vents," cheered Commander Trizzy.

"Oh really, what about meeting up with him?" said Gingerbread.

They all pause their struggling and notice Brian, Paul, and Steve packing up a X96 flight carrier aircraft on the loading dock of the school.

"He's going to escape!" screamed Cherry. Both Gingerbread and Commander Trizzy covered Cherry's loud mouth as they ducked back into the air vent.

Paul, Brian's right hand man, is the only one who noticed the noise Gingerbread, Cherry, and Commander Trizzy made.

"Hurry up, Paul, we do not have long until they find us," said Brain as he threw a backpack at his chest.

"We need to go," worried Steve. "Not until we get the weapons on board," demanded Brian.

"What do we do?" mumbled Cherry.

"Let's end this once and for all," urged Gingerbread as Cherry and Gingerbread began to lower themselves from the vent.

"Freedom," exclaimed Commander Trizzy as he hugs the ground.

After picking Commander Trizzy up off the ground they snuck near the X96 rolling from crate to crate. They all finally get close enough to Steve who stopped to take a break from lifting crates.

"Steve, watch out!" screamed Paul. Steve quickly turned around and noticed Gingerbread and Commander Trizzy. Steve headed for Paul as Brian began firing shots at them. Gingerbread and Commander Trizzy quickly begin to take cover back behind the crate.

"We need a weapon," suggested Commander Trizzy.

Gingerbread takes a metal pole near him and smashed the crate they were both leaning against. Loads of laser handguns began falling out of the crate. Both of them quickly grabbed one and returned fire.

After a few minutes of shooting, both sides began to run out of energy crystal ammo.

"Hey, this is pointless, Gingerbread," articulated Brian.

Suddenly, the entire floating institution began to tilt and created a steep angle forcing everyone to grab something to hold on to.

"Get to the ship, Paul and Steve!" screamed Brian.

"Oh no you don't," declared Commander Trizzy.

Due to the increasing angle, the Institution of Learning was falling. Neither Gingerbread or Commander Trizzy could make it to the ship in time. As Gingerbread and Commander Trizzy watched, Brian flew away on the ship.

Cherry comes up behind them. "Put these on, hurry!"

Unfortunately Gingerbread was unable to put his on in time and grabbed onto Cherry. Unlike Gingerbread, Commander Trizzy put his parachute on in a few seconds and was falling a few feet ahead of them.

"We are too heavy!" screamed Cherry.

"You better not drop me! Just pull the chute," shrieked Gingerbread.

"How do I do that?" yelled Cherry struggling to overcome the noise from the wind.

Eventually Gingerbread reached over and pulled Cherry's chute for her. They both began to float down along with Commander Trizzy somewhat nearby.

"What do we do now, Gingerbread?" asked Cherry.

"Yes, what do we do now?" asked Commander Trizzy.

"We survive," conveyed Gingerbread.

All three of them began to watch Brian's ship fly farther and farther away as the first sun began to rise in the night's sky.

www.ingramcontent.com/pod-product-compliance
Lightning Source LLC
Chambersburg PA
CBHW060123260626
47160CB00005B/1998